LARKSPUR
and the
GRAND MARCH

Ann Bryant & Debbie Boon

For Mickey Moo with love
And for Liz Morris's 'Animal' boys in 5th class,
St Mary's Place, Dorset Street, Dublin
M.A.

To my mum for loving my
work and me
D.B.

First published in Great Britain 2003
by Egmont Books Ltd.
239 Kensington High Street, London W8 6SA
Text copyright © 2003 Mary Arrigan
Illustrations copyright © 2003 Debbie Boon
The author and illustrator have asserted their moral rights.
Paperback ISBN 1 4052 0592 X
10 9 8 7 6 5 4 3 2 1
A CIP catalogue record for this title is available from the British Library.
Printed in Dubai

Contents

Red Bananas

Tum Ti Ti TUM!

Davy liked visiting his Aunt Becky. Her apartment was full of CDs, which she played really loud. Every day, and for a big part of the night, Aunt Becky played music on her CD player. That suited Davy just fine because he liked all kinds of music — even the kind that had fiddles and trumpets instead of electric guitars and seriously noisy drums.

'Tum ti ti tum,' Davy and Aunt Becky sang as they danced around in time to the music.

'I like the way you play it so LOUD, Aunt Becky,' he said.

'Well, there's no point in playing good music at a whisper,' said Aunt Becky.

It has to be loud!

But the neighbours didn't agree. They banged on their walls and said very rude things indeed. But Aunt Becky and Davy just went on singing and dancing. They couldn't hear them with all that loud music.

What a racket!

My poor ears!

One day, Aunt Becky opened the newspaper.

'Look at that, Davy,' she said. 'The Opera House people are putting on a great opera called *Aida*. How I'd love to go, but I can't afford a ticket.'

'Why don't we stand outside the Opera House?' said Davy helpfully. 'We might hear some of the music, if they play it loud enough.'

'What a brilliant idea!' cried Aunt Becky. 'That's exactly what we'll do. We'll go along later and stand outside. But first we'll go to the zoo because the sun is shining.'

A Cultured Lion

Davy loved lions. He leaned over the barrier and watched them as they paraded about in their enclosure. All except one, that is. He sat near the barrier looking very bored. Now and then, he yawned, showing his shiny sharp teeth, and gave a great sigh. Davy felt quite sorry for him.

Yaawwnnn!

'Come on, Davy,' said Aunt Becky, 'lots to see yet before we go to the opera.'

As Davy turned to follow her, he heard a voice saying, 'Psst. Hey, sonny.' But there was nobody about. Then he heard it again. 'Over here, boy.'

Very creepy thought Davy. Then the bored-looking lion stood up and pointed to himself with his paw.

'It's me, Larkspur,' he said. 'Are you really going to the opera tonight?'

Yoo-hoo, yoo-hoo!

Davy was so surprised to hear a lion talking to him that he lost his voice. He just nodded.

'Oh, lucky you,' said the lion. 'I would give my whole mane to go to an opera.'

'You would?' said Davy, finding his voice again.

Did I hear you say OPERA?

'And my tail as well,' said Larkspur. 'I positively adore opera. All that trilling and tum-ti-tumming.' He gave another sigh.

'I only get to hear snatches of opera on Tommy the Keeper's radio. I'm a very cultured lion, you know. Not like this lot in the zoo.'

'You can come with us,' said Davy. 'We can't afford tickets, but we're going to stand outside and listen. I'll just tell Aunt Becky.'

Friends for Tea

'Of course he can come with us,' said Aunt Becky, not at all surprised that a talking lion wanted to come to the opera. 'But first we must get him out of the zoo. I just happen to have my wirecutters in my bag. Isn't that lucky?'

Here they are!

While Davy kept lookout, Aunt Becky cut
a hole in the wire of the lions' enclosure.
The lions looked up in surprise as Davy
and Aunt Becky crawled through the hole.

'Look folks, dinner and dessert,' said
Ma lioness.

'Dessert looks nice,' said her daughter,
slobbering.

The lions padded towards Davy and Aunt
Becky.

'Growwwlll,' said Pa lion. 'Growwwlll.'
This annoyed Aunt Becky. She poked
him on the nose with
her umbrella.

'Get back, you greedy, moth-eaten thing.
One more step and you're a hearth rug.'
'GROWWWLLL,' said Pa lion even louder.

'Paws off, Pa!' said a deep voice. It was Larkspur. He had washed his mane and was looking very elegant. 'I'll thank you not to eat my friends. They're taking me to the opera.'

See you all later.

His mother shook her head. 'I might have known,' she sighed. 'My son, loopy Larkspur! The only lion I know who would prefer to listen to screechy people than to eat them.'

Hairy Beast People

'You'll need a disguise,' said Aunt Becky to Larkspur. 'People might get nervous if they see a lion going down the High Street.'

'Perhaps if I wore sunglasses?' suggested Larkspur.

Your mane would give you away.

What about a false beard?

'No good,' said Davy, 'you'd bump
into things.'

'You can hide under my big cloak,' said
Aunt Becky. 'See? I wore
it especially for
the opera.'

Larkspur fitted fairly well under Aunt Becky's cloak . . . only *fairly* well. As they passed along the High Street, people were very surprised to see four hairy paws walking along beside Aunt Becky's high-heeled shoes.

'Monsters,' someone whispered. 'Come to squash us!'

'Hairy Beast People!' said another. 'Come to eat us.'

'Aliens!' cried someone else. 'Come to take over the earth! Call the police!'

Really, These Humans!

Meanwhile, Aunt Becky was having problems.

'My poor corns,' she said. 'These silly high-heeled shoes are hurting my feet.'

'Why don't we take a taxi the rest of the way?' said Davy.

'Good idea, lad,' replied Aunt Becky. And so she put her fingers in her mouth and gave a really shrill whistle. 'To the Opera House, my good man,' she said to the taxi driver who pulled up. 'We're going to the opera, my nephew and me.'

Pheeewww!

24

She didn't mention that they were going
to stand outside the Opera House. And she
certainly didn't mention that there was
a lion under her cloak, even though he
was an opera-loving lion.

'Try to look like you're a furry rug,' Davy
whispered to Larkspur as they settled into the
back seat of the taxi. Larkspur put his fluffy,
maned head on Aunt Becky's lap and tried
to look like a furry rug.

'You're not a singing lion by any chance, are you, Larkspur?' asked Aunt Becky. 'I couldn't cope with a singing lion trying  to sing along with the tenors and sopranos.'

'Of course I'm not a singing lion,' said Larkspur. 'I'm not a weirdo, you know.'

'We're going to listen to *Aida*,' said Davy. 'It's pronounced Aaa-eee-da. It's about a soldier in Egypt long ago who falls in love with a poor and pretty girl called Aida. There are lots of songs.'

'There usually are lots of songs in operas,'

said Larkspur. Really, these humans! Did they think he was some kind of dumb animal?

'Anyway, I know all about *Aida* – and I know how to pronounce it. And I know that Aida is really the daughter of a king. I can tell you the whole story!'

'What a cultured lion you are!' said Aunt Becky.

'Yes,' said Larkspur. 'I certainly am.'

There was a lot of traffic in the street, and
Larkspur got bored with the way the taxi was
stopping and starting.

'Yawwwnnn,' he opened his mouth very
wide. It was just at that moment that the
taxi driver looked into his mirror and saw
the furry rug's enormous teeth.

'Yeeeeeeaaaaaaggghh!' he yelled, and
slapped into the car in front, which in
turn slapped into the car in front of that.

There was a lot of smoke and noise. Aunt
Becky was annoyed.

'We might as well walk the rest of the
way if people are just going to go bashing
into one another like that,' she said. She threw
a five-pound note through the window to the
quivering taxi driver. 'You silly little man,' she
said, pushing Larkspur under her cloak as
they all set off towards the Opera House.

'Help! Police!' shouted the taxi driver when he found his voice. 'There's a lion running wild in the street! Help!'

'Hello, hello,' said Constable Potts. 'What's all that shouting about then? Did you see the monsters, hairy beast people, and aliens too?'

'No, but I saw a lion,' cried the taxi driver.

'A vicious, ferocious lion!

And a ferocious lady

and her nephew!

Do something quick!

They're heading for the Opera House. We'll all be chewed up!'

I Wish We Had Tickets

By now, Aunt Becky and Larkspur had reached the Opera House. There were lots of people in their very best glittering clothes standing around in the foyer.

Nearly there, Larkspur.

'We'll just stand in the foyer too,' said Aunt Becky. 'We can pretend that we're rich and have tickets. And when all those people go to their seats, we'll just slip out again and listen from outside the door.' She sighed. 'I wish we had tickets.'

And in they went to mingle with all the glittering people who were chattering at the tops of their voices.

'Sounds just like the monkey house in the zoo,' muttered Larkspur.

'Shhh, Larkspur,' said Davy. 'And keep out of sight.'

The Signor is a star.

Here, here.

But Larkspur was so excited about being in a real opera house that he couldn't resist having a little peek. He gasped when he saw the splendid decorations and fancy wallpaper all around the foyer. Then he spotted the life-size poster of Signor Singalotti, the famous opera star.

Oh, Larkspur! You daft lion!

'Signor Singalotti!' he exclaimed,
forgetting that he was supposed to stay
hidden. With a howl of delight, he bounded
across the foyer to look at the poster up close.
'Oh, Larkspur!' cried Davy.

'Now there'll be trouble,' said Aunt Becky.

And, of course, there was. Lots of trouble.

For a moment, the opera lovers gazed in
amazement at the very large lion who was
kissing the poster of Signor Singalotti. Then,
with cries and yells, they scattered. They
climbed on top of
the booking office.

Who brought the LION?

They swung from the chandeliers. They climbed on to the statues of famous composers, and they tried to crawl under the very expensive carpet.

No Lions at the Opera!

'Hello, hello,' panted Constable Potts, rushing into the foyer. He was out of breath from running. 'Where's this lion then?'

'Over there,' shouted the manager as he swung from a chandelier. 'Catch him, officer.'

Constable Potts looked at Larkspur and backed away. 'You catch him,' he said to the manager. 'It's your theatre.'

'Does anyone have a gun?' asked the box-office lady who was crouching behind a statue of Mozart.

'Don't be daft,' said Davy, putting his arm around Larkspur. 'He only wants to hear the opera.'

'That's right,' said Aunt Becky. 'He even knows the story of *Aida* and some of the songs.'

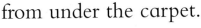

'We can't have a lion at the opera,' said the manager. 'Where would it all end?'

'Tigers at the ballet,' said the box-office lady, holding on to Mozart's ears.

'Pandas at concerts,' said the doorman from under the carpet.

'Positively no!' said the manager. 'Get a vet and a net and get that lion out of here.'

'What's going on?' said a very big voice.
Everyone turned to see a big bearded
man sweeping into the foyer.

WHAT is all the noise about?

'It's Signor Singalotti!' they
whispered in awe. 'He's singing
in the opera.'

Has someone phoned for a vet and a net?

'What is going on?' asked Signor Singalotti again.

'It's that there lion,' said the manager, as he swung to and fro.

It's that lot!

'He wants to see the opera, if you don't mind!' scoffed the box-office lady.

Signor Singalotti frowned and looked at Davy, Aunt Becky and Larkspur. Then he began to smile.

The Grand March

From the very best box in the Opera House,
Davy sat patiently through all the songs and
all the fiddle and trumpet bits of *Aida*.

'Is it nearly time for the Grand March?'
he asked, because he knew that the Grand
March is a very important part of the opera.

'Very soon,' whispered Aunt Becky.

And then it happened. The music got
importantly loud as people in Egyptian
costume began to march on stage. It was
a splendid sight.

'Will it be now?' asked Davy.

'Yes, now,' said Aunt Becky.

Davy leaned forward in the box. A beautiful lady led Larkspur on to the stage. His mane was all brushed and fluffed and he wore a jewelled collar around his neck. When the singing reached its loudest, the conductor nodded at Larkspur who put back his splendid head and roared.

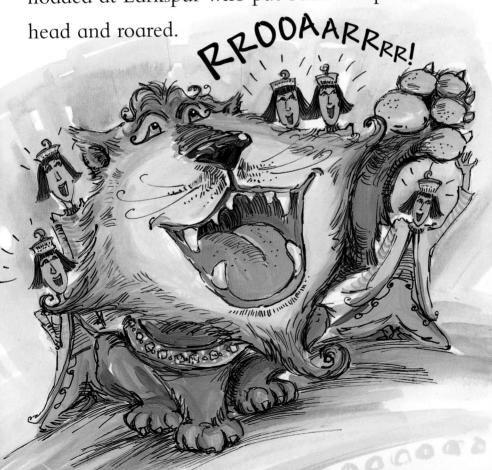

RROOAARRRR!

'Oooh,' gasped the audience. 'The Grand March from *Aida* has never been so grand!'

And they all stood up and clapped.

'That's my friend Larkspur!' shouted Davy proudly.

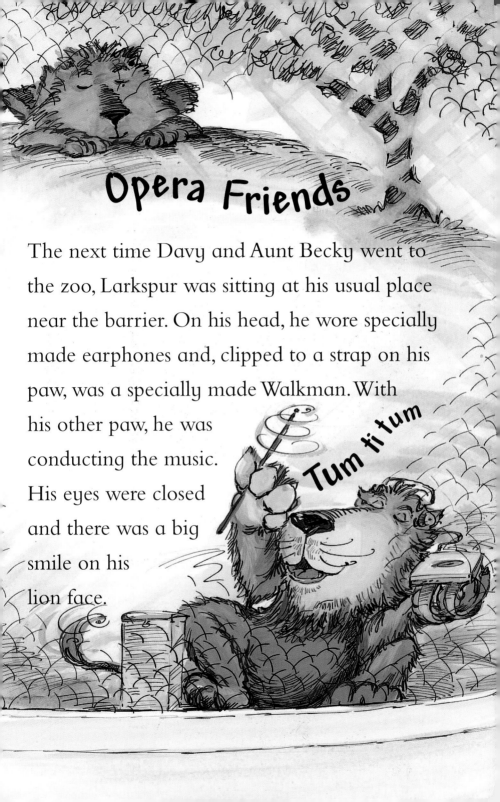

Opera Friends

The next time Davy and Aunt Becky went to the zoo, Larkspur was sitting at his usual place near the barrier. On his head, he wore specially made earphones and, clipped to a strap on his paw, was a specially made Walkman. With his other paw, he was conducting the music. His eyes were closed and there was a big smile on his lion face.

Tum ti tum

'Yoo-hoo, Larkspur,' shouted Davy.

Larkspur opened his eyes and grinned when he saw his opera friends.

'Look,' he said, pointing to the Walkman and the collection of CDs in a special waterproof box. 'A present from Signor Singalotti. Now I can listen to music all the time – thanks to you.'

'You deserve it,' said Aunt Becky. 'You were splendid.'

'Better than splendid,' said Davy. 'You were magic.'

'Yes, I was,' agreed Larkspur. 'And, most of all, I got to hear the opera from the inside.'

'And we got to hear it from a posh box,' laughed Davy. 'Thanks to Signor Singalotti.'

On the plaque that gave all the information about the lions, an extra bit had been added on. It said . . .

AFRICAN LIONS

LARKSPUR ~
STAR OF THE
GRAND MARCH IN
AIDA AND HONOURARY
MEMBER OF THE
OPERA COMPANY.